VAMPIRATES
DEAD DEEP

This book has been specially written and published for World Book Day 2007.

World Book Day is a worldwide celebration of books and reading. This year marks the tenth anniversary of World Book Day in the United Kingdom and Ireland.

For further information please see www.worldbookday.com

World Book Day is made possible by generous sponsorship from National Book Tokens, participating publishers, authors and booksellers. Booksellers who accept the £1 Book Token themselves fund the full cost of redeeming it.

Also by Justin Somper

VAMPIRATES: Demons of the Ocean
VAMPIRATES: Tide of Terror

And, coming soon . . .

VAMPIRATES: Blood Captain

VAMPIRATES
DEAD DEEP

JUSTIN SOMPER

SIMON AND SCHUSTER

SIMON AND SCHUSTER
First published in Great Britain in 2007
by Simon and Schuster UK Ltd
A CBS COMPANY

Copyright © 2007 Justin Somper
Chapterhead illustrations copyright © 2007 Blacksheep
Cover illustration copyright © 2007 Bob Lea

www.vampirates.co.uk

Simon & Schuster UK Ltd
Africa House, 64–78 Kingsway
London WC2B 6AH

A CIP catalogue record for this book is availabe
from the British Library.

ISBN-10: 1-416-93240-2
ISBN-13: 978-1-4169-3240-6

1 3 5 7 9 10 8 6 4 2

Typeset in Garamond by M Rules
Printed and bound in Great Britain by
Cox & Wyman Ltd, Reading, Berks

www.simonsays.co.uk

For Sally,
who has helped me swim up from the depths many times.
This one's for you!

The following events take place between the end of
VAMPIRATES: DEMONS OF THE OCEAN
and the beginning of
VAMPIRATES: TIDE OF TERROR . . .

Attention, first-time voyagers with the
VAMPIRATES crew! You do not need to have
read the previous books to enjoy VAMPIRATES:
DEAD DEEP . . . so go ahead, dive in!

CHAPTER ONE

Shore Leave

"Forty-eight hours!" said Bart, with a grin.

"Two whole days and two whole *nights*!" beamed Jez.

Together, the young pirates cried, "Shore leave!" before high-fiving each other, low-fiving each other and whooping.

Their friend, Connor Tempest, shook his head with a grin. At fourteen years old, he was one of the youngest pirates on board their ship, *The Diablo* – but that didn't stop his friends wanting to lead him astray at every opportunity. He knew how excited they were to have shore leave, in spite of being dedicated members of Molucco Wrathe's crew. "There's only one thing better than being a pirate on a pirate ship," Jez had declared as they'd sailed away from *The Diablo* a few hours earlier, "and that's being a pirate on shore leave with time on his hands and gold in his purse!"

Neither Jez nor Bart had stopped grinning since they'd set off from *The Diablo* in the small boat. Now, Connor calmly steered them into a cove crowded with ships, while Bart and Jez jumped up and down like excited kids, causing their craft to rock dangerously.

"So," Connor called across to them, "is this the place?"

"This is it!" Bart said, "*Calle del Marinero* . . . the strip of sin!"

"Erm, that's not exactly a *literal* translation," Jez said.

"Quite so, Mister Stukeley, quite so," said Bart, clearing his throat. "A literal translation would be . . . the Street of Sailors."

Connor looked up at the steep and inhospitable ridge beyond the mass of ships. Daylight was fading fast and the land was looking darker and more forbidding by the minute.

"Where exactly *is* the street?" asked Connor. "Right now, all I can see is a rocky outcrop. I thought you said this place was crowded with bars and taverns and stuff. How long a walk is it going to be when we get on land?"

"Are you blind, Mister Tempest?" said Jez. "Look around you!"

"We're not going on *land*," said Bart. "*This* is *Calle del Marinero* – right here. It's a floating city!"

As he manoeuvred their small boat through the mass of ships towering above them, Connor looked more closely at the other vessels. They were crowded with people and strung with lights. Music was blasting out – a deafening cocktail of rock, folk and thrash-shanty. He felt a charge of excitement. The boats themselves were the taverns!

Ahead was a regal junk, each of its red sails bearing the silhouette of a bird in various stages of flight. As they sailed nearer, Connor read the name on the side of the ship – *The Bloody Parrot*.

"Ah," said Jez, with awe, "*The Bloody Parrot*! I heard that its crew sailed in one night for a look-see and never left!"

"We'll have a drink there later," said Bart.

"We'll have a drink on *every* ship later!" said Jez.

Connor shook his head. He could see how this shore leave was going to shape up. Who knew what state Jez and Bart would be in by nightfall on Sunday? That was when *The Diablo* was due to pick them up from *Calle del Marinero*.

"Aw, don't look so worried," Jez said, ruffling Connor's hair.

"No, no, Mister Tempest," added Bart, "we shall take good care of you!" He climbed up onto the side of the boat. "After all, we are – are we not? – the Three Buccaneers?"

Connor nodded. A fellow pirate, Cutlass Cate, had come up with that nickname and it had stuck.

"One for all . . ." cried Bart, his voice booming over the music drifting down from *The Bloody Parrot*. From its top deck, curious revellers paused to look for a moment at the pirates' small bark.

"And all for one!" cried Connor and Jez.

At last, Connor spied a mooring slip and eased the boat expertly up to the wooden pier.

"Nicely done!" cried Bart, jumping down onto the wooden gangway and making light work of the requisite knots.

Jez dragged Connor off the boat and onto the pier. "Don't dawdle! We only have forty-eight hours!"

Connor found himself propelled along the jetty. It soon joined up with others, forming a boardwalk grid. Jez and Bart strode purposefully forth but Connor was slower, his eyes racing to take it all in. In every direction, the floating taverns competed for his attention – *The Saucy Sailor, Poseidon's, The Cannon and Cutlass* . . .

One small boat was even a floating tattoo parlour. Connor paused for a moment to watch the tattooist in action. He had always wanted a tattoo. At the boat's entrance was a series of flags, displaying the various designs. Wouldn't it be cool if the Three Buccaneers got matching tattoos? He saw an image of three cutlasses. Now, *that* would be perfect!

"Hey!" he called after Bart and Jez, but they were already disappearing into the thronging crowd.

"Hey yourself!" called a young girl just ahead of him, her ruby ringlets bobbing in the breeze.

She turned and Connor saw that she was actually an *old* girl – a *very* old girl. Her ringlets were an ill-fitting wig, her face was thickly caked in powder and her false eyelashes were as long and thick as a tarantula's legs.

"I'm Rose," she said, smiling at him and revealing an insufficient allocation of teeth. "Wild Rose, they call me. Wanna know why?"

"No time!" cried Jez, running to Connor's rescue. "No time at all! Now, come on, Mister Tempest. We must stick together!" Connor gratefully allowed himself to be dragged along the boardwalk.

"That was a close call," laughed Jez. "Better take care, young Tempest. There's all kinds of danger in *Calle del Marinero!*"

"Hey guys, whaddya think about this?" Bart was up ahead, standing by the gangway to a beautiful old junk. Connor saw its name painted on the side of the boat in silvery script: *The Dirty Dolphin*.

Bart was pointing to a painted sign...

Arm-wrestling contest tonight.
Commences 7:00 pm sharp!
Last man at the table wins free beer and yabbies!

"Yabbies!" said Connor. "Yum! Count me in!"

"Remind me," said Jez, "what *are* yabbies?"

"In or out-and-move-it-along, lads?" roared a bouncer at the foot of the gangway.

"In!" exclaimed Bart, striding up the gangway.

"In!" chorused Connor and Jez, following close behind.

Connor's pulse was racing. One thing was for sure – the Three Buccaneers were in for an adventure or two before their shore leave was up!

CHAPTER TWO

The Contest

The deck of *The Dirty Dolphin* was only dimly lit. Connor's eyes took some time to adjust to the gloom.

"Where do we sign up for the contest?" he heard Bart say.

Bart and Jez were talking to the barman – a thickset guy in a singlet. An inky school of dolphins swam down each of his arms. Even the barman's fingers were tattooed, just below the knuckles. D-O-L-P-H. Connor decided it must be the barman's name.

"You're a little late," said Dolph. "Contest's been going an hour already."

"But we've only just got here!" said Bart.

The barman threw him a grin. "Well, hey, if we'd known *you* were coming, buddy, we'd have waited." He smirked. "Don't stress it. You can still enter. No need to sign up. Just throw a dollar in the pot and get in line. I reckon Kal's about ready for some fresh competition. Seen off just about everyone else tonight."

"Kal?" said Bart. "Who's he?"

"Don't ask, don't tell," said the barman. "That's the way

we do things around here. Don't get a lot of regulars. People breeze in and out on the tide."

Bart threw three dollars in the pot. Then he turned back to Dolph. "Looks like Kal's luck is about to change. Us three pirates ain't going home with empty bellies tonight!"

"Yeah, right," said Dolph. "Contest is in the back bar. Just go through those doors there."

"Thanks," said Bart. "You might want to put some yabbies on to heat."

Dolph fixed him with a smile. "They heat up quick enough," he said.

Bart led the way through the saloon-bar doors. Beyond was a smaller, gloomier bar, though not so dark you couldn't make out the faces of the other customers as they turned to check out the three newcomers. Connor could read the looks they were getting. They said, "Think you've got a chance, boys? Well, think again!"

In the centre of the room was a small wooden table. Before it was an empty chair. Behind it was Kal. His face was bowed so that all that was visible was his hair. It was neatly cropped and bright blue. Suddenly, Kal looked up at the three newcomers, stopping them dead in their tracks.

"You're a girl!" exclaimed Bart.

"No flies on you, mate," said Kal. The other customers roared with laughter and drummed their feet in approval. "Friends call me Kally," she said, her eyes sparkling as blue as her hair.

What kind of trick is this? Connor wondered. Kally was wearing a singlet, which revealed strong shoulders and muscled arms. But, really, there was no way she could

7

challenge them in strength . . . was there? Could it really be true that she'd already seen off every other challenger in *The Dirty Dolphin*? There was only one way to find out.

"So boys . . ." Kally was suddenly all business. "Who's first?"

"That'll be me," said Jez, stepping forward. Connor gave Jez a squeeze on the shoulder. "Good luck!" he said. Jez winked and sat down.

Kally set her elbow on the table and reached out her arm. Jez did the same. Their hands met.

"Ready, fella?"

She didn't talk like any girl Connor had met before. He was warming to her. And he could see Bart was also watching her intently.

"I'm ready," Jez said.

It was over even before it had started. Kally powered Jez's arm down onto the table without flinching.

There were snorts of derision from the lowlifes gathered in the bar. "Thought we'd get a proper match that time," moaned one old fart, before hiccupping loudly and falling onto the floor.

"Nice try, mate," said Kally, smiling sweetly as Jez got up from the table, dazed. "Who's next?" she asked.

"Me," said Bart, sitting down opposite her. He towered over Kally but that only seemed to amuse rather than intimidate her.

"Brought in the big guns, eh?"

Bart said nothing, simply resting his elbow on the table and tensing his bicep.

It was no contest. Straight away, Bart had Kally's arm almost horizontal on the table. Connor grinned. All his buddy had to do now was press Kally's flesh into the wooden table.

But that proved easier said than done. Although she was just millimetres away from defeat, Kally's hand held steady. Her face gave nothing away either. There was no sign of effort there at all.

Suddenly, Bart's arm began to move. In the opposite direction!

This can't be happening, thought Connor. *Kally's staging a comeback!*

Bart held firm but the strain was easy to read in his face. A few seconds later, Kally powered Bart's arm down onto the table.

Bart pushed back his chair, stunned. "You're strong, man!" he said.

"Thanks, man!" said Kally, with a wink.

As Bart stepped back from the chair to rejoin the others, Dolph appeared with a tray full of drinks. He gave Kally a smile. "Looks like you're making short work of these pirates."

"Pirates, eh?" she said, intrigued. She turned to Connor as he stepped forward to take his turn. "Aren't you a little young to be a pirate?" she asked.

"I'm fourteen," Connor said. "Old enough."

"He's one of the best swordsmen on the ship," Bart added, proudly.

"So he should have a strong grip," said Kally, her eyes alight. Connor sat down, his face flushed. *Was she laughing at him?* Her eyes really were incredibly blue. He felt mesmerised by them, as though he was being dragged down into unfathomable depths.

9

"Ready?" Kally asked.

Connor gripped tightly onto her hand. "Ready," he said.

He felt immediate pressure from Kally. She was strong. Very strong. But so was he. Not as strong as Bart, for sure, yet he seemed to be standing firm against her. For now, at least.

As the battle continued, the crowd around the bar hushed, realising that they might finally have a match on their hands.

But Connor didn't look at the crowd. He kept his eyes on Kally's blue gaze, not even watching their hands as they waged war against each other. Connor had the advantage. He could sense it. Maybe Kally was at last tiring, after a night of defeating all-comers. Connor felt elated. How cool would it be for *him* to defeat Kally and stand his buddies a night of beer and yabbies to celebrate their shore leave?

Suddenly, Connor felt Kally's hand pump with fresh energy. It was pushing his own backwards. Had his attention slipped? Maybe she had only been toying with him. He pushed back with renewed vigour. They were holding each other off now, as evenly matched as two opposing magnetic currents.

Then Kally pushed through. Connor forced all his power into his own palm but he was unable to hold off the assault. He could feel the table just below his hand. It would be over in five seconds, four, three, two . . .

But Connor had hidden reserves of energy too. Over the years, in all the sports he'd played, he'd learned how to dig deep just when it looked like it was game over. He became aware of his hand forcing back Kally's. Connor was unsure where the strength had come from but he could feel it

10

growing and consolidating within him. He was pushing back Kally's hand and there appeared to be nothing she could do about it. This time, he was sure there was no trickery. Kally's strength had finally given out. He gave one final push and her hand hit the table. He was so surprised, he forgot to let go.

"Congratulations," she said. "Looks like I'll be paying for my supper, after all."

Connor was dazed. He kept staring at Kally's hand, unable to believe that he had beaten her. She had defeated every last challenger in this dingy back bar . . . but one.

"Good going, buddy!" cried Bart, slapping him on his back.

"Yeah," said Jez. "Well played, Connor! Looks like you've saved the day . . . or, rather, the night!"

Across the table, Kally gave the lads a wink. "Well, that was fun, boys," she said, "but now it's time for this gal to fly."

"Wait!" Bart said. "Stay. Have a drink with us!"

Kally smiled but shook her head. "I have to get back to Lorelei," she said. "I've already been gone too long."

"Who's Lorelei?" said Bart. "Your sister?"

"Not *who*," said Kally, "but *what. The Lorelei* is my boat. The others will be waiting for me."

Bart wasn't about to let her go without finding out more. "What kind of boat is it?" he asked.

She considered his question for a moment. "I guess you could say we're a dive-boat."

"Diving," said Bart, nodding. "I love to dive."

"Everyone loves to dive," said Kally, her blue eyes sparkling.

"Just stay for one drink," Bart pleaded.

"Sorry, mate – not even for you." Kally smiled but shook her head. "The others are waiting."

Bart looked crestfallen. Kally turned and called into the crowd. "Will someone get me my chair?"

A gap opened up in the murky darkness and through it came a chair, wheeling its way towards Kally. She turned and put out a hand to slow the spinning wheels. Then she pulled the wheelchair close beside her and eased herself swiftly into it. Now Connor saw that Kally had no legs – at least, no visible legs. They were hidden in an oilskin bag, fastened at the waist with a cord. That explained her exceptional upper body strength, he thought.

Kally propelled herself away from the table, then glanced back and smiled at the dumbstruck lads.

"Gentlemen, it was a great pleasure making your acquaintance," she said. "I surely hope we'll run into each other again."

With that, she winked and spun her wheels, disappearing into the bright lights of *Calle del Marinero*.

CHAPTER THREE

Brawl

"Her eyes were *so* blue," Bart said, sighing again. "What would you call that shade of blue? Azure?"

Jez gritted his teeth. "Mate, you met her for a few minutes and you haven't stopped talking about her for over an hour—"

Bart went on, oblivious. "Maybe aquamarine?"

Jez rolled his eyes at Connor. "There really aren't enough free yabbies in the world to make me want to listen to this." He reached his hand across the bar and squeezed Bart's shoulder. "Mate, play another record. *Please!*"

"Actually," said Connor, "that's not such a bad idea!" He glanced over at the jukebox in the corner of the bar. The old Wurlitzer had been pounding out thrash-shanty ever since they had arrived. After a time, the music felt like a severe assault on the eardrums.

Connor slipped down from his bar-stool and walked over to the jukebox. He took a coin from his pocket and surveyed the music choices. There had to be something better than this racket! But, flipping through the pages, it seemed like *The Dirty Dolphin* had just about every

13

thrash-shanty anthem ever laid down, and not much else besides.

At last, he saw a tune he quite liked – *Cape Cod Girls*. It was one of his sister Grace's favourites. Song B17. Connor slipped his coin into the slot, raised his finger and punched in B, then 1 . . . But, before he had the chance to punch the 7, a long white finger crowned with a bruised nail jabbed the 9.

"Hey!" Connor cried. His words were drowned out as the same thrash-shanty began blaring. *Not again!* Connor turned around, his face dark as thunder.

He was facing a tall, thin boy, not much older than himself, dressed in worn black leather. The boy's lank hair was as dark as his clothes and hung low over his face, obscuring half of it. The half that was visible was pale and waxy, with a smattering of acne and a small purple scar. On his pale lips, a nasty cold sore had taken up residence. The lad looked positively vampiric but, as he opened his mouth, Connor was assailed by the stench of garlic.

"What's wrong?" said the boy. "Don't you like my taste in music?"

Connor shook his head. "It stinks," he said. "As much as you. That was *my* money. It was my turn to choose."

The lad grinned. "Should have been quicker, then, shouldn't you?"

Connor had had enough. He reached for his rapier, which hung in its sheath at his waist. Drawing the sword out into the light, he smiled at the lad. "I reckon I'm quick enough, thanks all the same."

The boy seemed unfazed by the sight of the sword. He reached his own hand into his trouser pocket and removed a flick-knife, opening it up as casually as a cigarette lighter.

Connor shook his head, amused. "Going to fight me with that, are you?"

The lad's one visible eye looked into Connor's with disdain. "Oh, I'm not going to fight you at all." He clicked his fingers. Suddenly, two men appeared at his side. To call these guys "hulks" was to do them a disservice – they were huge. They too were dressed in worn leather. Each brandished a razor-sharp rapier.

"Yes, Master Moonshine?" said one.

"You called, Master Moonshine?" said the other.

The lad frowned. "I told you to drop the 'master', remember?" He turned back to Connor. "These two will fight you." He raised his flick-knife, extending the merciless blade to Connor's neck. "*I'll* just swing in at the end to finish you off." Connor winced. Moonshine smiled and stepped back, allowing his goons clear access to Connor. "Make it swift but painful," he said to them.

Connor stood in front of the jukebox, his mind racing. How come these big guys were commanded by this runt? And, of more pressing concern, how was he was going to get away from here with all his vital organs intact . . .?

He didn't have to worry for long.

"Step away from the jukebox!" boomed a voice. "That's right, Tweedledum and Tweedledee, I'm talking to you!"

Connor smiled. Bart to the rescue! His shipmate was standing behind the two thugs, his broadsword raised.

But the thugs didn't move.

"Let him go!" rasped another voice. Connor saw that Jez had Moonshine in a half-nelson. The poor lad could hardly get out his words. "*Let him go!*"

15

At their master's words, the henchmen backed away from Connor.

"That's it," said Bart. "Nice and easy and my friend won't spoil Moonstruck's pretty face." He smiled. "Though really, it could do with a bit of work, I reckon."

Connor let out a breath and gripped his sword, back in attack mode.

"Right," said Bart. "And now for the complex manoeuvre I like to call . . . legging it!"

He hurdled the bar, with Connor and Jez hot on his heels. Moonshine's goons were too surprised to give chase immediately. Instead, they turned gormlessly towards their master. Moonshine was bent double, hands on knees. Nevertheless, he managed to yell. "What are you waiting for? Get after them! Mess 'em up!"

By now, Jez and Connor were through the bar doors and back out on the deck of *The Dirty Dolphin*. Bart was already halfway down the gangplank.

"Phew," said Connor, as he and Jez caught Bart up. "That was close!" He grinned. "One for all and—"

A roar of fury from the deck interrupted him. The two flunkeys were giving chase.

"Come on, boys," said Bart. "We're out of here!"

The three pirates ducked down onto the pier.

Just then, something whistled past Connor's ear. Dazed, he looked up as a circle of metal took root in the wooden pier, one step ahead of him. As he got close, he saw it was a vicious-looking multi-pointed blade.

"A starfish *shuriken*," said Jez, grabbing Connor.

"Where did it come from?" Connor asked.

"Up there, by the looks of things!" Bart said. He pointed

16

up to the deck of *The Dirty Dolphin*. There was Moonshine, his face almost luminous in the darkness. He raised his hand and, suddenly, another *shuriken* whistled through the air, aimed directly at their heads.

"What now?" Connor asked.

"What do you reckon?" Bart said. "RUN!"

Connor needed no further encouragement. The three pirates raced along the pier, as a third blade sailed over their heads.

"He must be gaining!" Jez rasped as they ran. "Who *is* that guy?"

"Trouble," said Bart. "That's who."

"Talking of trouble," Connor said. "What do we do *now*?" He pointed two metres ahead to where the pier ran out. All that lay beyond was cold, dark water.

"Quick! Up here!" Bart cried, hanging a right and racing up the gangplank of another tavern. Jez and Connor ran after him onto *The Bloody Parrot*.

The tavern crowd turned as the three strangers thundered onto the deck. Suddenly, out of the throng emerged two familiar figures dressed in black leather – Moonshine's men.

"Of all the gin joints in *Calle del Marinero* . . ." cried Bart.

"*Now* what?" cried Connor as the thugs lurched towards them.

"Follow me!" cried Jez, jumping up onto the side of the ship. He leaped over the edge, landing on the craft moored at its side.

Connor followed and heard Bart's footsteps behind him. There was no time to waste. Moonshine's men were hot on their heels.

17

"Keep running!" Bart called, racing across the deck. As he did so, he used his broadsword to cut through the sails and rigging to make their path easier. Confused revellers dived out of the melee and raced to the ends of the ship.

A now familiar whistle hovered above them. Another *shuriken*!

"Duck!" commanded Bart as the spinning blade shot past them.

They had run out of ship again, but there was another tavern vessel moored next to this one. Together, the Three Buccaneers launched themselves off the side and onto the next boat. As they jumped through the air, Connor couldn't help but smile. Even in the midst of danger, he was strangely enjoying himself – his best buddies on either side. But, as they landed, there was no more time for smiles. Moonshine's thugs were gaining on them once again.

Bart sliced through the sails. This time, instead of racing away, the people on deck turned and drew their own swords, angry at having their party interrupted. The boys were getting some ugly looks. Connor could see the edge of the ship but, this time, there seemed to be nothing but ocean beyond. Had they really reached journey's end?

He looked desperately at Bart and Jez but they were equally flummoxed. Then two things happened. First, Moonshine's henchmen arrived on the deck, drawing attention away from Connor and his buddies. Then, another *shuriken* sailed through the air and landed like a dart in the ship's mast.

"Jump!" cried Bart.

As they sailed through the air, Connor readied himself for the icy waters below. Instead, he hit wood. They had landed on another boat, much lower and smaller than the ships on either side. And, Connor realised as he staggered to his feet, it was moving.

Looking up towards the deck they had jumped from, he saw Moonshine's men gazing down at them in frustration. Already, too much water had opened up between them to jump across. A final *shuriken* sailed through the air, missed its mark and descended into the ocean; though not before spearing an unfortunate seagull.

Connor let out a long breath. The seagull's fate could so easily have been his.

"That was close!" Jez said, as he and Bart stood up, brushing themselves down.

"Well, you guys certainly know how to make an entrance."

The voice was familiar. So too was the girl who wheeled her chair along the deck towards them.

"Welcome to *The Lorelei*," she said. "You know, I had a feeling I hadn't seen the last of you."

Bart looked at Kally and beamed. "Aquamarine," he said at last. "*Definitely* aquamarine!"

CHAPTER FOUR
The Lorelei

"Couldn't stay away, huh?" Kally beamed at the pirates. "Well, it looks like you're with us for a spin out to the reef, tonight."

Connor glanced around *The Lorelei*. A small windjammer, its hull sat low in the water, as it rocked gently on the ocean. Its billowing lateen sails shimmered silver-blue in the moonlight. The boat was strung with lanterns and there was the sound of chatter and soft, sweet singing. The deck, however, was much quieter and more sparsely populated than that of *The Diablo* or, indeed, *The Dirty Dolphin*.

"Come and meet the rest of the crew!" Kally whizzed over to the centre of the deck, coming to a standstill beside four of her crewmates. Like Kally, they were all in wheelchairs. They were gathered around an upturned chest, which was covered in playing cards.

"Everyone," Kally announced. "Meet my new friends." She beamed. "Three of the finest young pirates who ever roamed the ocean . . . *if* you believe what *they* say." She winked. "Guys, this is Diani, Teahan, Lika and João."

There was a lot of hand-shaking and high-fiving while they introduced themselves and, before they knew it, the lads were being offered drinks, quizzed about where they'd come from and invited to join in the card game. Kally's crewmates were clearly bursting with as much energy as she was. And they were all young and fit. Like her, they kept their legs bound tightly in oilskin bags, with only the upper parts of their body visible. Dressed in a variety of tank-tops and sleeveless shirts, it was easy to see that they were all strong, with the same well-developed shoulder and arm muscles as Kally. Connor certainly wasn't about to challenge any more of them to an arm-wrestle.

"Welcome, friends," said João, when everyone had a full glass. "Welcome aboard *The Lorelei*."

"OK, you've met these reprobates," said Kally, when they'd finished their drinks. "Now it's time you met Flynn."

"Who's Flynn?" asked Connor.

"Flynn," said João with a smile, "is our esteemed captain."

Connor already had the feeling this was a rare kind of boat. No crew-member would dare to say to a stranger arriving on *The Diablo*, "Come and meet Molucco." He was always referred to as Captain Wrathe. But then, this wasn't a pirate ship. And *The Lorelei* was far smaller than *The Diablo*.

"How many people are in your crew?" Connor inquired, as the pirates followed Kally along the deck towards the stern.

"Counting Flynn, there are thirteen of us," she said. "Unlucky for some, eh? As you can see, boys, *The Lorelei*'s not the largest of boats, though she suits us just fine."

21

Connor heard a sudden screech of wheels. One of Kally's crewmates was racing down the deck, straight towards her. Connor winced, preparing for disaster but, at the last second, Kally swerved, expertly avoiding a collision. "Happens all the time," she said, with a grin, "Any more wheels on board and we'd be gridlocked!"

"How do you cope with the sails and rigging and stuff?" Connor asked as they moved past the central mast. "I mean . . ." He couldn't work out the most diplomatic way to ask the question.

"You mean from our chairs?" Kally said lightly. "Well, there's a lot we can do from deck level." She paused so they could see another of her crewmates adjusting the tilt of one sail, manipulating the rigging from below with ropes as if they were the strings of a kite.

"Nice one!" said Jez.

They had almost reached the boat's stern. Up ahead was the steering deck. *The Lorelei* had been adapted so ramps replaced stairs to the raised platform.

"I need a little bit of a run-up to this," said Kally, spinning her wheels furiously, then propelling herself forward, straight up the ramp.

"Well, what do you reckon?" said Bart to the others.

"It's an awesome boat, isn't it?" Connor said.

"I'm not talking about the boat, doofus! I'm talking about Kally. Isn't she amazing?"

"She's great," Connor agreed, seeing a warning look in Jez's eye. Bart caught it too.

"Look, don't worry, guys," said Bart. "It's not like I'm going to do anything crazy. I'm just saying she's a really cool girl, that's all."

"Okey-cokey," said Jez. "Then let's follow her up to meet the captain, shall we?" He gestured for Bart to go first.

Then Jez grabbed Connor's shoulder and pulled him towards him. "Word to the wise," he hissed. "When Bartholomew Pearce tells you he's not about to do anything crazy, that's a very good indication that he's about to do something crazy."

Connor smiled. What exactly could Bart do? They were only having a tour of *The Lorelei* and a drink with their new friends.

"Come on, slowcoaches," called Kally from the raised platform. "Or do I need to get you some wheels to keep up with me?"

Connor and Jez marched up the ramp. They joined Bart as Kally wheeled forward to the very back of the boat.

"Flynn, I brought some people to see you."

"People? What kinda people?"

The first thing they saw was the back of his chair. The support was carved to resemble the curve of a fish's tail, disappearing into the waves.

The captain turned to get a look at them. He was older than the other members of the crew, with a face weathered by the ravages of time and a life at sea.

"Connor, Bart and Jez," Kally said, "it's my great pleasure to introduce you to Flynn, a.k.a. Captain of *The Lorelei*." She dipped her head and smiled, before adding, "a.k.a. my dad."

Connor saw Bart straighten up a touch as he leaned forward to shake Flynn's hand. As Connor shook hands, he looked into the captain's face and saw his resemblance to Kally. Like her, his eyes were blue – but they were a paler, milkier hue. In the moonlight, his hair seemed silvery-blue like hers but, on second glance, was actually pure white.

Then Connor noticed something he hadn't clocked before. Though Flynn was in a chair with wheels on its feet, it wasn't a wheelchair like the other members of the crew had. Nor was his lower body bundled, like theirs, into an oilskin bag. Instead, he wore coarse linen trousers and his bare feet rested on the deck, quietly tapping a rhythm as he spoke.

"He's not disabled!" Connor exclaimed.

At once, the others turned towards him.

"Ahhh . . . I didn't actually mean to say that," Connor said, mortified that he'd spoken aloud. Bart's face was thunderous. Connor turned to Kally. "I'm *really* sorry," he said. "I didn't mean anything . . ."

Kally shook her head and smiled. "No sweat, Connor. It can be a minefield being around us. No, Flynn's not disabled."

"Sir," said Bart, changing the subject, "Kally said that this is a dive-boat?"

"What's that?" Flynn said, his thoughts evidently elsewhere.

"Diving, Dad," prompted Kally.

"Oh, diving." He twisted around once more. "Yes, yes, the kids love to dive."

Connor smiled at the way Flynn called the other crewmembers "kids". Though Kally seemed to be the Captain's only actual child, he obviously took a similarly paternal attitude to the rest of the crew.

"So, how did you get into diving?" Connor asked.

"I come from a line of sailors," said Flynn. "My father was a captain and his father before him. Diving was always our business. There isn't a dive spot from Cozumel to Christmas Island I don't know like my own footprints. But when my Kalypso was born, things changed. She was different . . . special!"

Flynn reached out a hand to his daughter's cheek. She turned her face and softly kissed his palm. "Others would have sheltered her – kept her safe ashore – but that would have been like clipping the wings of an angel. My Kalypso . . . she may need wheels to move about on land but, in the water, she can fly."

Connor wondered what he meant by that, but Flynn continued. "We're the kind of people who keep ourselves to ourselves," he said, "but even so, word gets around. Others came to us, other exceptional kids like Kalypso. I took them aboard *The Lorelei*. It wasn't hard to adapt the boat for them. They handle ninety per cent of the sailing themselves and I just step in when I'm needed. Which, to be honest, is getting less and less."

Kally shook her head. "That's not true, Dad." She turned to the others. "Dad thinks he's getting too old to be captain – that he needs to retire soon."

She looked sad, suddenly, and her eyes lingered on Bart for a moment. Then she smiled, changing the subject. "So, you've heard how we all came to be aboard – now, remind me, how did *you* three come to be on board?"

Bart looked embarrassed. "You might say we got into a little hot water after you left *The Dirty Dolphin*."

"Really?" Kally was clearly amused. "Well, we're on our way out past the reef. We could turn tail and drop you back

25

in the harbour, if you like. Or you could hang out with us a while. We're heading to a major dive site."

"Oh?" Connor said. "Whereabouts?"

"It's called Hell Bay," Kally said, her eyes aflame. "Though it's more heaven than hell. It's not far from here. It's incredibly beautiful. There are fire shells and pygmy seahorses and really rare blue-ringed octopi . . ."

"It sounds amazing!" said Bart.

"That's a great invitation, Kally," said Jez, jumping in, "but we need to stay around *Calle del Marinero*. We have to rendezvous with *The Diablo* here at sunset on Sunday."

"That's two days from now, Jez!" Kally said. "We can be there and back by then, easy."

"Sounds perfect!" said Bart, enthusiastically.

Connor had to agree. He'd far rather spend his time away from *The Diablo* diving and chilling out with the crew of *The Lorelei* than back in one of the floating taverns of *Calle del Marinero*. And he was certainly in no hurry to run into the thrash-shanty loving, *shuriken*-wielding Moonshine and his goons again.

"Come on, Jez," said Bart. "Where's your sense of adventure, mate?"

Jez shook his head, but his anxious expression dissolved into a smile. "OK, I'm in."

"Excellent!" Kally said.

Flynn turned his attention back to the steering wheel, and began guiding the boat out of the harbour mouth, leaving *Calle del Marinero* far behind.

There was something special about the moment when you left harbour, thought Connor. It wasn't just about leaving the land for the ocean. It was about disconnecting from all the fixed points in your life and heading out into a world where everything was fluid. It was a heady sensation and one to which Connor Tempest, at fourteen years old, was already an addict.

CHAPTER FIVE

Night Swimming

"Hey, I think I'm getting the hang of this!" Connor said, discarding his last card and holding up his empty palms.

Jez shook his head and raised his eyebrows, while Lika threw down her own hand of cards in mock disgust.

"Beginner's luck," laughed João, his eyes sparkling in the lantern-light. It appeared to be easy sailing out towards the reef. The waters were calm tonight and the stars were bright enough to guide the way. Flynn was back at the helm, steering their course, while Diani and Teahan had been assigned the task of manning the lateen sails – listening for Flynn's shouts and occasionally adjusting a line of rigging here and there.

For the rest of the crew, the only imperative appeared to be to relax. It seemed to be second nature aboard *The Lorelei* to just sit and watch the world pass by. It wasn't hard to feel at home here. Connor already felt an easy and familiar camaraderie with the crew – especially Lika and João, with whom he and Jez were engaged in an increasingly competitive bluejack contest. Meanwhile, Bart and Kally were sitting together, deep in conversation, at the bow of the boat. Connor could see their silhouettes through the cloth of the sails.

"They make a good pair, yes?"

Connor looked up to find João nodding his head towards Kally and Bart. Connor smiled in agreement.

"I've never seen Kally look so happy," said João. "I think perhaps Bart will have to stay on *The Lorelei* for ever." He laughed.

"Maybe we all will," said Jez. "I can tell you, mate, it's a lot more chilled here than on our ship."

"Really? But you're pirates!" said João. "You need adventure, excitement, danger, no? I think life aboard *The Lorelei* would bore you."

Jez leaned back in his chair and stretched out like a cat. "You know what, pal? I think I could handle some boredom. I've been a pirate since I was knee-high to a sea-urchin and it feels great to take some time out."

João smiled. "How about you, Connor? Is that how you feel?"

"Connor's only been on *The Diablo* for five minutes," said Jez. "Besides, his sister's on board. He couldn't abandon her, could you, mate?"

"No." Connor shook his head, firmly.

"They're twins," Jez explained.

"Really?" Lika said, staring at Connor with increased interest. "They say that twins have a special bond, that they can communicate with each other without speaking and stuff. Is that true?"

Connor shrugged. "I don't know if it's quite like that, but Grace and I certainly pick up on each other's moods."

"Really?" said Lika. "So tell us then, can you sense what Grace is thinking right now?"

"I doubt it," said Connor.

Lika smiled at him. "Try."

Playing along, Connor shut his eyes. The others remained silent. He summoned up an image of Grace, as he'd last seen her, watching him climb into the light-boat and leave *The Diablo*. He focused on her face. Her mouth was open and she was saying something. He couldn't hear the words. He had to find a way of getting closer.

He thought of the locket which he'd given her and visualised her wearing it, hoping that would intensify the contact between them. It worked!

Suddenly, he heard the words she was speaking.

Danger. Underwater.

He was shocked at the clarity of the vision. Was it a true vision or merely a trick of the mind? He kept his eyes shut tight and found that Grace seemed even closer now. He could see the anxiety in her eyes and hear the words even more clearly.

Danger. Underwater.

Connor's heart began to race. Opening his eyes, he found the other three staring at him curiously.

"What is it?" asked Lika.

"She spoke to me," Connor said.

"Really? What did she say?"

Connor took a breath. As he tried to relax again, he made a decision. "She said . . ."

"Come on, mate," said Jez. "Out with it!"

"She said . . . they're rubbish at cards so be gentle with them!"

30

Connor could feel Lika and João's eyes on him – there was a moment's silence, then they both burst out laughing.

Time passed swiftly as they played game after game of bluejack. Then Flynn's voice called out from the stern. "We're here!"

"We're here!" Kally echoed, excitedly racing down towards the centre of the boat. Bart jogged alongside her.

Within moments, the entire crew had wheeled down to the centre deck. The pirates sat down amongst them. The crew seemed to be waiting for something . . . or some*one*. All eyes turned as Flynn stepped down from the steering platform and made his way slowly along the deck towards them. He walked erratically, a soft boot-step on the deckboards with one foot, then a heavy thump with the next. Out of his chair, the captain's age was all the more evident.

As he joined the others, his weathered face broke into a smile. "It's a beautiful night for a swim," he said. "And a wonderful spot for it, eh?"

The crew of *The Lorelei* all looked at him, their eyes eager and expectant. The full moon bathed their faces in pure light. Connor watched, fascinated.

"Well, what are waiting for?" Flynn said. "It's time to go and explore the reef! Who shall be first, tonight?"

His eyes roved around the deck and settled upon Lika. He nodded and she steered her wheelchair out of the crowd, towards the very edge of the boat. She sat there for a moment, looking out at the sea. Flynn came over and placed a hand on her shoulder. He was humming a strange tune. Suddenly, Connor noticed the oilskin bag which bound Lika's legs start to move – gently at first, then more strongly. It was almost as if Flynn was bringing Lika's legs back to life.

"Are you ready?" Flynn asked her gently.

Lika nodded. As she did so, she took her hands to her waist and unfastened the bag. It fell away in her hands, revealing not legs but a vast, oily fish tail, which thumped the deck as if relieved to be free at last.

It was as natural to Connor as it was unbelievable. It was as if he had known all along that *The Lorelei* was no ordinary dive-boat. Now he watched in wonder as Flynn lifted Lika into his arms and carried her towards the side, before releasing her to plunge into the waters below.

Flynn smiled, turning to the others. "Who's next?"

Now it was João who joined Flynn. Once more, Flynn hummed the haunting tune. Once more, Connor watched as movement stirred beneath the oilskin bag. Then João tore away the bag and, with Flynn's help, launched himself off the side of the boat. He soared into the air, before disappearing beneath the surface of the water.

One by one, Flynn called each of his crew forward and delivered them to the ocean. At last, there were twelve empty wheelchairs on deck and only Connor, Bart and Jez sitting silently amongst them.

Flynn beckoned them. "Come," he said. "We'll watch them from the stern."

They followed, silently, a few metres behind the old captain, as he made his way back up to the steering platform. Joining him at the wheel, they glanced down.

The waters were dark for a moment. Then João and Lika swam into view. Their tails, which had been dull and monochrome up on deck, were now ablaze with light, illuminating the water all around them.

"Aren't they beautiful?" Flynn said, his face bathed in the reflective glow.

"They're . . . they're mermaids!" Bart said, dumbfounded.

Flynn smiled, extending a long bony arm around Bart's shoulder. "I don't think João would take too kindly to being called a mermaid, do you?" He chuckled. "Around here, we call them *fishtails*. They're *my* fishtails. My beautiful fishtails!"

He gazed down and Connor's eyes followed his, watching with wonder as the jewel-coloured lights shot back and forth beneath the surface of the water.

"Let's go in with them!" said Bart, his eyes shining with the possibility. He turned to Flynn. "That's all right, isn't it, sir?"

Flynn smiled, nodding.

Connor, Bart and Jez stripped down to their underwear and dived off the side of the boat. As Connor hit the water, it was dark. Then, suddenly, it was illuminated by laser brightness. He looked down and saw Lika and João swimming beneath him. He watched as Bart swam over to Kally. Just as Flynn had said earlier that day, she was like an angel underwater. They all were. They swam with such effortless grace, it made Connor feel clumsy.

"Welcome to our world," said João, swimming over to meet him, the reef glowing coral-pink behind him.

"We're so glad that you all came," said Kally, beaming.

Connor looked at Bart and Jez in surprise. So the fishtails could talk underwater. Connor wondered if he too

33

might be invested with these magical powers. He opened his lips to speak, but found himself swallowing a mouthful of salt water.

Kally smiled at him. "This is our world," she said. "Just as we are restricted above the water, so you are beneath it." She smiled. "But you're very welcome as our guests."

With that, she dived down below him, her tail sending a rainbow of light up in her wake. Connor wished that Grace could be here to share this with him. Remembering the message she had sent him, he tried to send one back to her – to let her know that she was wrong, and that everything was OK.

Magic. Underwater.

He repeated the phrase several more times in his head, hoping that it would get through to her – that somehow she might see this amazing sight for herself. Then he dived down deeper, following the coloured lights to join his good friends, old and new.

CHAPTER SIX

Fishtails

When the fishtails were at last done swimming, Flynn threw a rope line into the water. The boys, who had long since returned to the deck to dry off, watched as Flynn helped the fishtails back onto the boat. When Bart offered his assistance, Flynn shook his head. "Thanks," he said, a little sharply, "but I can still manage."

He carried each of the fishtails back to their chairs, binding their tails inside the oilskins once more. Connor watched as Flynn poured a little seawater into each of the oilskins before fastening them tightly. "Their tails must never dry out completely," he explained. He flipped a handle on each of the wheelchairs so that they reclined, almost like beds. Flynn shuffled off and pulled a pile of blankets out from a bench seat, then tenderly lay a rug over each fishtail. As if under a spell, all twelve of them already seemed to have fallen into a deep sleep.

"The shock of coming from their world into ours is tiring for them," Flynn explained. "They will rest now and, when they wake, their balance will be restored." He threw a blanket to each of the pirates. "Take these up to the foredeck," he said. "You can bed down there."

With that, he turned and disappeared off towards his seat at the wheel.

Connor slept soundly but woke anxious to check that he really was on *The Lorelei*, and that it hadn't all been a dream. He was pleased to find that not only was he still on board but that Jez was already awake.

"Mermaids!" said Jez. "Can you believe it? Mermaids!"

"They don't call themselves that," Connor said, speaking softly as Bart was still sleeping beside them. "Remember? They call themselves fishtails."

"Hmm," said Jez. "You say tomatoes and I say . . . mythological sea creatures we had no idea really existed!"

Connor grinned. "Well, they certainly *do* exist. Look at them!" He eased himself up into a sitting position and looked back along the deck at the fishtails, still sprawled over their chairs.

"Connor," said Jez, the tone of his voice suddenly changing.

"Yes?"

"I'm a tad concerned for our safety."

"Really?" said Connor. "You think there might be something fishy going on?" He smiled. "Sorry, I couldn't resist! Go on."

Jez smiled too but then grew serious. "I've been remembering the old myths, and traditionally merm . . . fishtails – whatever you call them, well, traditionally they lure sailors and take them prisoner."

"You think we're being lured here?" Connor asked, alarmed.

36

Jez shrugged. "I don't know. I mean, we're at sea, aren't we? And I might be wrong, but I reckon we've been sailing through the night. We could be miles away from *The Diablo* by now."

Connor looked over the side of the boat. Was Jez right? It was hard to tell. How could you tell one patch of ocean from another? "Maybe I'm being paranoid," Jez continued, "but I just can't shake the feeling that something's wrong here."

Connor frowned. He remembered his fleeting vision of Grace and her message to him. *Danger. Underwater.* Had she been warning him about the crew of *The Lorelei?* He still couldn't get his head around how she could know where he was, let alone that he was in danger. He wondered if he should share the vision with Jez. "Actually," he began, "there *is* something I wanted to—"

"Hey, what's up, dudes?" Bart's cheery voice drowned out his own. He sat up and thumped them each on the back. "How are my fellow Buccaneers this morning?"

"Concerned," Jez said.

"Concerned?" repeated Bart. "About what?"

"Mate, this isn't easy for me to say. I know you're getting on well with Kally and everything . . ."

Now Bart was frowning. "If you've got something to say, Jez, then please just spit it out."

"You remember what they say about merm . . . erm, fishtails?"

"That seeing them causes bad luck?" Bart didn't seem surprised by Jez's question. Perhaps he too had been pondering the myths.

Jez nodded. "That and more."

Bart shrugged. "Is that all? You're worried by a little maritime mythology? Life's more complicated than that, isn't it? I mean, think about Tempest's sister, Grace. She was kidnapped by Vampirates but they let her go. And, according to her, they actually looked after her. Isn't that so, Connor?"

Connor nodded. Then a shadow crossed his face as he remembered Grace's tale of her encounter with the evil Sidorio, and he shivered. Sidorio had imprisoned Grace in her cabin in an attempt to satisfy his bloodlust. The Vampirate captain himself had had to take extraordinary measures to rescue her from certain death. Grace had seemed very calm when she'd recounted the tale afterwards, but perhaps that was because Sidorio had been immediately banished from the ship and not heard of since.

Connor turned to Bart. "Yes, all but one of them."

"That's my point," Bart said. "We have to be open and judge everyone on his or her individual merits. There's good and bad in every group of people . . ."

"These guys aren't *people*, though, are they, Bart?" said Jez. "I mean, they have great big swishy tails instead of legs."

Connor thought Bart would be enraged by Jez's words, but instead he smiled calmly. "You can't write off a whole crew just because they're a little different." He smiled. "Look, they're waking up."

The others followed his gaze along the deck. One by one, the fishtails were pushing aside their blankets and bringing their chairs into the upright position. Their energy seemed to return to them instantly and they began chattering and laughing. Just as Flynn had predicted, their rest had returned them safely to the world above the sea. The boys watched as Kally turned and immediately began wheeling her chair towards them.

"Good morning, pirates!" she beamed. "How are you all doing?"

"Fantastic!" said Bart, beaming at her and reaching out his hand to hers. She took it and gave it a squeeze. Connor thought then that they looked like a couple who had been together a long time, not one who had met just the night before. Kally was great. Seeing her again, listening to her lively chatter, Connor was instantly brought around to Bart's way of thinking. Once you discounted the fish tail itself, Kally was just a regular girl. Well – a very beautiful, intelligent, funny, regular girl. It was going to be hard to leave *The Lorelei* when the time came – especially for Bart – but not because the fishtails wouldn't let them. They were a cool group of people and it was a great boat. Connor decided he was going to quit worrying and make the most of every last minute of his time aboard.

"Hey guys," cried João, joining them. "Come and get some breakfast!"

The day slipped easily away on board *The Lorelei*. After breakfast, the fishtails took another dip in the ocean. The young pirates joined them in the water. This time, as Connor swam beside them, it seemed second nature that his new friends had luminous fins and that they could talk underwater.

Back on deck, as Connor towelled himself dry, he asked when they would reach Hell Bay.

João smiled at him. "You're just itching to dive, aren't

you? Don't worry, we'll get there soon enough. In the meantime, there are plenty of ways to entertain yourself . . ."

Connor grinned. In contrast to his time on *The Diablo*, a day on *The Lorelei* was blissfully free of chores. He was free to while away the hours perfecting his bluejack technique, working on his tan, grazing on delicious snacks and chatting about everything and nothing with Jez, Lika and João.

Bart didn't join them. He spent the whole day with Kally. Whenever Connor caught a glimpse of them, they were talking or laughing together, like old friends. Or more than friends. Connor wondered how they had so much to say to each other but he supposed it was nothing more profound than the chit-chat that he was exchanging with the others.

Flynn sailed the boat smoothly across the ocean – so smoothly that, most of the time, you were hardly aware it was even moving. And yet, at last the sun gave way to dusk and the dusk to star-pierced darkness. Everyone gathered together for dinner and, afterwards, João strummed his guitar and Lika, Teahan and Diani sang shanties for their pirate guests. Connor watched as Bart took Kally's hand and held it in his own. When the song was over, the pirates clapped.

Jez and Connor went over to congratulate João. "Nice playing, man," said Jez.

João smiled at them. "Hey, do either of you play? No? I can teach you a few chords, if you like."

A little while later, Bart and Kally came over to join them. Bart put his hands on Connor and Jez's shoulders.

40

"Guys," he said, "there's something I need to talk to you both about."

"We'll let you three have a private chat," Kally said, indicating to João that he should follow her. Reluctantly he put down his guitar and the two of them wheeled away, leaving the Three Buccaneers alone.

CHAPTER SEVEN

Rift

"What is it?" asked Connor.

"It's pretty simple, really," said Bart. "I'm thinking that when you guys hook up with *The Diablo* tomorrow, I'm gonna stay here on *The Lorelei*."

Jez's jaw dropped. "You're *what?*"

Connor frowned. He could understand the temptation to remain on the dive-boat – especially given Bart's obvious bond with Kally – but even so . . .

"This is so sudden," he said. "I mean, all your life you wanted to be a pirate. That's what you told me, remember? My first night on *The Diablo?*"

Bart nodded. "I remember, buddy. Of course I do. But things change. People change. I'm not the kind of person who draws up lists of 'pros' and 'cons' before making a decision. I feel it in my gut. And, right now, my gut is telling me to stay here with Kally and the others."

"You can't do this!" At last, Jez was able to string a sentence together. "Connor's right – your whole life has been geared towards becoming a pirate. Eight years – *eight years ago*, we joined *The Diablo*. Are you going to throw all that away because of Miss Wonderwheels and a gut instinct?"

Bart gave Jez a dark look. "Don't call her that," he said. "And don't think for a moment that this was an easy decision. We've been talking about it all day. If I could split myself in two, I'd be a happy man. One Bart could go back with you to *The Diablo*. The other could stay here and help out Kally and Flynn."

"*Help out?*" Jez was incredulous. "What do you *mean*, help out?"

"Flynn's getting old," said Bart, "He's done an amazing job looking after the fishtails but every day he's losing strength. There's only so long he can go on as captain of *The Lorelei*. And, as independent as the fishtails are, they need someone to assist them. They can't survive on their own."

"Wow!" said Jez, shaking his head. "She's certainly worked her sorcery on you!"

"Sorcery?"

"How else do you explain it? You stepped onto this ship, not twenty-four hours ago, as a rational pirate and suddenly you're ready to give everything up for her!"

"It's not just about Kally."

"Come off it, Bart," said Jez. "I've known you way too long for you to pretend this is about a higher purpose. We all know you go weak in the presence of beauty. And Kally *is* beautiful. There's no doubt about that." He shook his head once more. "But she's a beautiful *mermaid*."

"They're *fishtails*," said Bart, surprisingly calmly.

"Call them what you want," said Jez, "fishtails . . . kulullu . . . naiads . . . nixes . . . It doesn't matter what you

43

call them. It all comes down to the same thing. They're half human and half fish and they lure sailors to their deaths."

"Even if that was true," said Bart, "she isn't luring *me* to my death. I'm not talking about *dying*. I'm talking about *living* – here, on *The Lorelei*."

Jez shrugged. "That isn't a life. Not for you. It's a living death."

As the pirates' words grew louder and more heated, Connor noticed that the fishtails had stopped what they were doing and wheeled their chairs along the deck. Suddenly, they were all around them. He exchanged an uneasy glance with João.

Bart and Jez stood in deadlock, their words and emotions spent.

Suddenly, Jez realised that he was surrounded. He looked around in anger. "Bloody mermaids!" he cried, pushing through the wheelchairs and marching angrily to the other end of the deck.

Kally wheeled over to Bart. He looked at her sadly, then back towards Jez.

"He'll come around," she said, squeezing his hand. "He just needs some time to get used to the idea. I promise, by the time we get to *Calle del Marinero* tomorrow, he'll have changed his mind. You'll see."

Connor looked along the deck. Jez was right up by the bow. He could go no further without jumping overboard. And, in the middle of the open ocean, that wouldn't be a clever option.

Connor glanced back at Bart. Could this really be the end of the Three Buccaneers? It might feel right in Bart's gut but Connor's gut told another story. Something was wrong on *The Lorelei*.

Once more, he saw Grace's face. He heard her warning. *Danger. Underwater.* Well, now he knew what that meant, didn't he? The danger was Kally and the others. They had lured Bart away from his friends, away from his pirate family. Connor didn't want to be forced into choosing sides but he had to go and comfort Jez. Bart had Kally now. Jez was on his own.

CHAPTER EIGHT

The Shark

Two fathoms below the surface of the ocean, Sidorio – the renegade Vampirate – takes his rest. It's a place as far removed from light as you can find on this planet. Darkness pervades his being here, seeping into his ears and nose and eye-sockets as intently as the water. Just as he likes it. Light can be such a menace. Others cling to the light; fear the dark. He smiles. How they would loathe it here.

And yet, many creatures prosper in this place. He is watching some of them right now – a school of hagfish. They feast on a chunk of whalemeat, helpfully discarded by a predator above. The hagfish barely merit the name "fish". No sleek shape for them. No glittering scales. They are more like thick worms – ill-formed creatures. All they are good for is feasting on the dead flesh of this world – flesh they don't even have the ability to kill for themselves. *Why, they don't even have teeth*, thinks Sidorio, running his tongue over his own golden fangs.

But what hagfish lack in aesthetics, they make up for in gumption. They may not have teeth but they suck flesh from bones at a pace that can make you nauseous to watch.

They may look vile but they are ruthlessly efficient. It's a combination Sidorio rather admires.

Now he watches as a new visitor arrives in these inky depths. A hammerhead shark. On paper, not much prettier than a hagfish but, thinks Sidorio, personality goes a long way. Sleek and knowing, the shark swims above the hagfish. The scavengers continue feasting until the very last moment. Then, they take their leave. No point in messing with a shark.

Sidorio watches as the creature dives in and takes a bite of the whaleflesh. Perhaps it isn't to her taste. Perhaps she was only proving a point. She leaves the rest of the carcass unbitten and swims on. The hagfish return to their business of sucking and chomping. It is what they know, what they are.

The shark comes towards Sidorio. He immediately recognises in her the arrogance of the few creatures who straddle both the dark waters below and the bright waters above. Sidorio reaches out a hand and she swims in, nuzzling it. Then she retreats back a touch, raising herself in the water. They are eye to eye now. Equals. *Yes*, thinks Sidorio, *you're right. We two* are *the same. We know both darkness and light. We can make our choices.*

He looks into her eyes and sees that she is in a playful mood. She swims up higher. He follows. It is as if she is calling him. As if, higher in these waters, there may be some sport to be had. Sidorio swims strongly in her wake. It is time to leave the dark waters behind him for a time.

He is in the mood for some sport.

CHAPTER NINE

Hell Bay

The waters of Hell Bay looked tranquil in the early morning sunshine. *We must have sailed through the night to get here*, thought Connor. Did Flynn never sleep? No wonder he looked so frail.

In spite of its name, it was a beautiful spot. Glancing around, Connor felt a deep sense of calm. Suddenly, out of the placid waters, sprang a pair of dolphins. Connor watched with delight as they swam along, leaping in and out of the water. There could be few better sights to wake up to than this.

But as the dolphins swam away, the events of the previous night flooded back. He glanced down and saw Jez, still tossing and turning in his sleep. On his other side, there was an empty space. Bart had not joined them on the sleeping deck last night. *It's happening already*, thought Connor. *We haven't even left yet, but already Bart's cutting the ties.*

Looking up, he could see the fishtails asleep on the deck, their chairs brought together and reclined in the centre. Bart was lying on a bench, not far from Kally.

Seeing this, Connor made a decision. They had to seize the moment.

"Wake up, Jez!" he whispered, nudging his friend.

"*Whaaat?*"

"Wake up!" Connor hissed once more. "And try not to make too much noise."

Jez opened his eyes, blinking in the light. "What time is it?" he asked.

"It doesn't matter," said Connor, urgently. "The fishtails are asleep. This is our last chance to talk to Bart alone, to make him see sense."

Jez nodded. Clearly the memory of last night was fresh in *his* mind too.

"Wait here!" said Connor. "I'll get him to come over."

He set off barefoot along the deck, trying not to make a sound. In a few paces, he was standing right beside the cluster of fishtails.

Gently but firmly, he reached out his hand to Bart.

Even before he touched him, Bart's eyes opened and his face greeted Connor with a familiar smile.

"Can we talk?" Connor whispered. "Over there?"

Bart nodded. "Sure, buddy," he said quietly.

He raised himself upright and together they walked back to the bow of *The Lorelei*. Jez held up his hand and he and Bart silently high-fived each other.

"I'm sorry, mate," said Jez, "for all those things I said last night."

"Me too," agreed Bart. "I've been going over them all night. Didn't get a wink of sleep. I never meant to hurt you guys – you're my best buds. You know that, don't you?"

Jez and Connor nodded.

49

"That's why we want to be sure you've really thought through this decision," said Jez.

"I have," said Bart, but there was something in the tone of his voice that made Connor think his mind wasn't quite as made up as his words suggested.

"How about we go back to *The Diablo*—" began Jez. Bart immediately started shaking his head.

"Wait," said Jez. "Please. Just hear me out! How about we go back to *The Diablo* and talk to Captain Wrathe about this?"

"Captain Wrathe?" said Bart.

"I'm sure he'd have some good ideas of ways to help these guys out," said Jez. "Don't you agree, Connor?"

Connor imagined the scene. Bart telling Molucco Wrathe that after eight years in his service he'd decided to break the binding articles that every pirate has to take to look after a ship of fishtails. He could imagine the interesting shades of red that Molucco's face would go as he considered Bart's proposal – and then instantly declined it.

"I think it's a really good idea to talk things through with Molucco," said Connor, calmly nodding. "He's not just our captain, Bart. Why, I've heard him say that he looks on you as the son he never had."

"Really?" Bart said, clearly surprised at this information. "Molucco said that?"

"Yes." Connor nodded. He felt really bad telling the lie or, at least, exaggerating the truth. But he'd stop at nothing to save Bart.

"Maybe I *have* been a little hasty," said Bart. "But you know me, guys! Sometimes my heart rules my head."

Seeing they were gaining ground, Jez gripped his friend's

shoulder. "There's nothing wrong with that, mate. We're all guilty of it sometimes. And Kally's a beautiful girl. I can see how she'd spin your world around."

Bart turned and looked back at her. Connor followed his gaze. He noticed with a shiver that the fishtails were waking up. Their time was running out. Even if they *were* successful in changing Bart's mind, he had an uneasy feeling that it wouldn't end there.

"These guys need me," said Bart.

Jez twisted Bart's face back towards them. "No," he said, gently. "They need *someone*. And we can help them find that someone. You're destined for greater things. For a ship of your own, a *pirate* ship . . ."

"Besides," said Connor, "*we* need you. Jez and me. Your friends. Your pirate family. Molucco and Cate. Can you imagine how upset Cate would be if she heard you'd gone away and not even said goodbye?"

"Cate . . ." said Bart, his face showing the impact of the name. Connor silently congratulated himself on this masterstroke, but there was no time to be complacent. Kally was upright in her chair now and looking over at them. Perhaps it was simply the way the light fell on her face, but Connor thought he saw a flicker of anger there. She turned, helping João with his chair, whispering something to him. Now, they both looked over at the three pirates.

Connor turned back to Bart. There was no more he could say. Ultimately, it was Bart's decision.

"Don't worry, buddy," said Bart. "I know what I need to do."

CHAPTER TEN

In Deep

"Wow!" Connor said, spotting a shoal of silvery fish swimming just below the ocean's surface. "The water's *so* clear here," he said. "I bet the diving is great!"

João laughed. "You'll find out soon enough! Think you're ready?"

"You bet!" Connor said, beaming down at him. He couldn't contain his excitement any longer. Even from the side of the boat, he could see the wealth of colourful sea-life waiting there for him. Sitting in his wetsuit, the sun beating down on him, Connor couldn't believe how well things had turned out. The Three Buccaneers were together again! The fishtails seemed to have taken Bart's change of heart in good spirits. Even Kally had said that she was cool with it. And Flynn had laughed and said that he wasn't ready to give up his captaincy just yet. It had all been a storm in a teacup — a storm brought about by the exhilaration of shore leave, perhaps, and the strange magic of *The Lorelei* and its crew.

"I can't wait to get down there," said Jez, coming to sit beside Connor, dressed in his wetsuit. "Should be pretty special, huh?"

Connor nodded. He was raring to go. They'd been working on their breathing all morning and he felt ready. It was called *pranayama* and was designed to slow your heart rate before your descent. The slower your pulse, the further down you were able to dive.

Bart came to join them. Kally wheeled her chair up alongside him.

"Kalypso!" cried Flynn from the stern. "Can you come up here for a moment?"

Kally shrugged and turned her chair around. "No rest for the wicked!" she said, giving Bart a friendly punch before whizzing off up the deck.

"She seems to have taken it really well," said Jez, zipping up his suit.

"We had a good talk," Bart said. "We'll definitely keep in touch."

He sat down by his friends. Together, they prepared themselves for the dive. As Connor followed João's precise instructions from the water, he could already feel his pulse starting to slow. His body was perfectly calm, though he was aware that deep at his core he was excited and fully adrenalised. The dive at Hell Bay was such a cool way to finish their weekend off!

He sat beside Jez and Bart, their flippered feet dangling over the edge of the boat. Beneath them in the water, two of the fishtails – Loic and Musimu – had swum down to the ocean floor to fix a weighted line.

"How deep is it?" Bart asked, as Loic surfaced.

"You don't need to know that," Loic replied, smiling. "This isn't about going deep. It's about discovering the water in a new way – discovering *yourself* in a new way."

"He's right," said João. "The most important thing is to keep your body and mind relaxed at all times. Don't push yourself to swim down too fast. Take it nice and slow to maximise your oxygen supply. Just follow the rope. We'll be close by." João nodded his head. "OK, one at a time – first Connor, then Jez, then Bart."

Connor looked at his comrades. Each extended their right arm and they touched hands in a fist.

"One for all and all for one!"

"OK," called Bart. "We're coming."

Connor slipped on his mask and duck-dived into the water. As he hit the water, he looked back up to see Jez jumping down to join him. But then he noticed Flynn come over to Bart. He said something Connor couldn't hear.

Bart called down to him. "I'm just gonna help Flynn with the mainsail. You guys start without me. I'll follow you in a jiffy."

Connor gave him the thumbs-up. Suddenly, a shaft of sunlight fell on a circle of water in front of him. To his amazement, he could see Grace's face. Her eyes were fixed upon him intently as she spoke.

Danger. Underwater.

This was getting silly. It wasn't Grace. It couldn't be. It was just his nerves getting the better of him. He'd be fine. He knew it. João, Loic and Musimu were there to *help* him. There was nothing to fear. He had to keep calm. Once more, he repeated the breaths in and out.

His flippers disturbed the surface of the water and the image of Grace disappeared. Connor shook his head to clear it, then spat into his mask and wiped it clean. He slipped it over his face, then dived down into the water, finding the top of the weighted line.

"That's it, Connor," came João's reassuring voice. "Take your time. Melt into the water."

Connor no longer found it strange that he could hear João's voice underwater. All he knew was that its tone was incredibly calming. He found himself easing into a natural rhythm. He reached his arms along the rope, heading down. As his body relaxed, everything felt different. He could feel the slow but regular thud of his heart and every muscle – from the top of his head down to his toes – as if he truly was at one with the water. Perhaps this was something close to what it felt like to be a fishtail.

"Well done!" said João encouragingly at his side. "If you want to let go of the line now, you can."

Connor looked at his hands on the rope, just above the weight. There was no time to dither. He released his hands and swam a few strokes. João drew up alongside him. "Very good," he said. "Your lung capacity is unusually strong."

They must be deeper than twenty metres now. The waters here were bluer than ever. A stingray was serenely floating just ahead of his nose.

"Stay calm," said João. "She won't do you any harm. You belong here now, just as much as she does."

Together, they observed the rare grace of the stingray. Connor felt as if he'd been granted access to a new world. It was amazing to think that he'd spent all these weeks above the surface of this very ocean. Up there was only half the story.

Suddenly, he felt a pressure in his lungs. He frowned. He didn't want this to end. Not yet. Instantly, João was at his side. "It's OK, Connor. It's nothing to worry about."

That's easy for you to say, thought Connor. His head was pulsing with warning signals.

"Just another metre or two," urged João. "You can do it! You're nearly at the ocean floor."

Connor hesitated. They said that the body was sometimes stronger than the mind gave it credit for.

"Concentrate on your breath," João said in his soothing tones. "Think how good you'll feel when you reach the bottom!"

Connor saw a bright yellow shoal of clownfish sweep past him. He couldn't stop now. He reached down the line, pulling himself deeper.

"That's it, Connor," said João, encouragingly. "Just another couple of metres."

Out of the corner of his eye, Connor saw that Loic had come to join them. Was everything OK? Shouldn't Loic be with Jez? Or had Jez gone back up already? Perhaps his lung capacity wasn't as strong as Connor's.

"It's all right," João said, sensing his anxiety. "Everything's fine, Connor. Don't stop now!"

But Connor suddenly sensed everything was *not* fine. Even before he saw Jez — his eyes shut, his body limp — being carried still deeper by Musimu. As he registered the sight, Connor felt hands firmly grip him on either side, forcing him down.

"Come on, Connor," said João, in the same steady voice. "Do you want to go deep . . . or do you want to go *dead* deep?"

Suddenly Connor saw the ocean floor. But any sense of achievement he might have had was overcome by a cold flood of fear. The fishtails hadn't brought him and Jez down here to perfect their dive technique – they had brought them here to remove any obstacles to Bart staying on *The Lorelei*. They had brought them here to kill them! Did they really need a new captain that badly?

But the plan was fatally flawed. Bart wasn't stupid. He wouldn't stay with Kally if he knew the fishtails had murdered his best friends. Only it wouldn't seem like murder, would it? It would just be a terrible accident. Connor could imagine how convincingly João would break the news – his sad eyes wet with tears as he told how, in spite of his and Loic's pleas, Connor and Jez had overstretched themselves . . .

Connor's heart started to race – the very last thing he could afford at this point. He felt the pressure of João and Loic's hands on his shoulders. Ahead of him, on the ocean floor, lay an ominous sight – a skeleton, a circle of chains and, in the dead mariner's hands, a rusting sword.

"Look!" João said with a laugh. "You're not the first pirate to reach the ocean floor!"

Connor received the words with horror, finally realising the depths of João's betrayal.

"It didn't have to end like this," João said, as though reading Connor's thoughts. "You could have just let him go. You don't need another pirate. But we won't survive without another captain."

So you're going to kill for one? Connor wanted to speak, but opening his mouth now would only speed up his death. Instead, he just shook his head slowly, hoping that João could see the hate in his eyes.

"Don't look at me like that," said João. "I'm only doing

my best for my crewmates. Just like you would for yours."
He smiled. "One for all—"

"And all for one!" added Loic. The two fishtails
chuckled. It was a horrible sound.

Connor's eyes were half closed now. He had managed to
slow his breath, in spite of his terror, but there was a limit
to how long he could survive.

"He's losing his air," Loic said. "Leave him. The job is
done. We have our new captain."

"It's a shame really." Connor heard João's receding voice.
"He was kind of a fun guy. The other one too. And it was
good to have some decent opposition at cards."

As Connor's eyes embraced the darkness, he felt his back
bump against the seabed. Suddenly it was deadly quiet. The
fishtails had swum off, perhaps to check on Jez. Connor
thought of his buddy. Was Jez hanging on in there or had
he succumbed to the worst already? Connor tried to shut
out the fear for a moment.

Not for the first time in his life, he found himself facing
death underwater. Cheng Li, the pirate who'd saved him
from drowning then, had told him it was a gentle way to
die, but he didn't plan on sticking around to find out
whether she was right. Thinking about Cheng Li gave him
an extra surge of energy. She was a fighter – *she* wouldn't
give up. Not even under these circumstances. He could
imagine her talking to him now. *Did I rescue you, boy, only
to have you drown once more, at the hands of mermaids?*

He opened his eyes and found himself face to face with
the skeletal remains of the dead pirate. His eyes fell to the
rusting sword held loosely within the skeleton's fingers. *I'll
just borrow that*, he said to himself, reaching out for the hilt.

Grabbing it from the skeleton's clutches was easy – as if the dead sailor was lending him a hand from beyond the grave. Now the hard work began. Moving the sword through the water was far from easy. It took an extreme effort and Connor knew that he had little strength left. The only possible way to get back to the surface alive was to conserve his energy, to keep hold of his breath for as long as he could.

With a grim sense of determination he began swimming, the sword gripped tightly in his right hand.

Loic stopped his ascent and turned to watch Connor struggle up from the sea-floor.

"He's certainly got stamina," Connor heard João say.

João's sneering tone gave Connor even more determination. The fishtails were swimming back towards him now, but they were in for a surprise. As Loic homed in on him, Connor pulled the immense weight of the sword through the water.

But he was too slow. Loic laughed and easily swerved out of danger. "Let the pirate swim with his rusty sword," he sneered. "It'll sink him before it saves him." Connor wanted to cry out in frustration. He had no fight left, and almost no breath. With or without the sword, he'd never make it. He was going to die. Here, in this pirate's boneyard. He thought of Grace. She'd tried to warn him and he hadn't listened, hadn't taken heed. Now, he'd never see her again.

Suddenly the waters around him bubbled, then revealed the shape of another diver. Slowly, a familiar face came into focus. It was Bart! He had come to rescue him!

With an encouraging smile, Bart grabbed the sword

from Connor's hands. He propelled himself forwards fast, lifted the sword and sliced through João's tail.

There was an ear-piercing scream. Then the waters filled with dark blood. And then, all hell broke loose.

CHAPTER 11

End Of

At João's anguished cries, the other fishtails swam to his aid. The sword had sliced through the tip of his tail and he was rapidly losing a terrible amount of blood. It flooded the water like red smoke.

Bart grabbed Connor's now unconscious body and, letting the bloodied sword drop to the ocean floor, began to swim powerfully up, past the fishtails and into clearer water.

Beneath him, the sword floated slowly back into the hands of the skeleton pirate.

The fishtails circled around João as his truncated tail flapped out of control. Its trail of blood acted as a clarion call to a trio of hammerhead sharks swimming close by. Scenting a kill, they swam into the heart of the red mist, their hunger fully roused.

Some of the fishtails fled to the surface at once, but Loic and Musimu stayed on, holding their bleeding comrade between them, frozen with indecision.

The sharks closed in fast, their teeth sharp and merciless. They didn't stop to consider the unusual shapes of the fish they attacked. Loic and Musimu could only save themselves. At last, they released João's limp body to the rapacious jaws.

Above them, Bart swam strongly towards the surface, wondering how much time he had before Connor's breath finally gave out. Jez was surely already dead. He couldn't dwell on this thought. Instead, he focused solely on his and Connor's survival and powered on. His own air supply was weakening, but he wouldn't give up. He owed his buddies.

Below him, the sharks had made light work of their first prey. Now they circled Loic and Musimu thoughtfully, as a new predator swam forward to join them. Nature has a hierarchy and, just as hagfish give way to sharks, so the hammerheads gave way to the newcomer.

Sidorio swam closer, registering the confusion in Loic and Musimu's eyes as he approached. He knew what they were thinking. *How could a man come to be here? And why did the sharks not attack him?* But, like them, Sidorio was neither man nor fish. As they would find out soon enough.

The waters were thick with João's blood now. The scent of it overcame Sidorio and, before the fishtails' horrified eyes, he changed. His pupils became pits of fire, no remnant of humanity left in them. And, when he opened his mouth, his two gold fangs seemed as alarming as a whole row of shark's teeth.

There was no possibility of escape.

Bart heard the screams from below as his head finally broke the surface and he felt the breeze on his face. He pulled Connor up alongside him – he was still unconscious. He had to get him back onto the boat. Bart looked up towards *The Lorelei*. Two people were staring down at him.

"Help us up!" Bart rasped, barely able to speak.

Neither Kally nor Flynn moved. It was as if they hadn't heard him.

"Come ON!" Bart pleaded. "João is dead, Loic and Musimu too. There are sharks down there. Help us up!"

Still Kally and Flynn remained motionless.

"Please!" Bart cried. "Connor's unconscious and I can't find Jez. Please! I was prepared to give up everything for you. I still could. If you have any humanity at all, please let us up onto the boat."

Even now, Kally and Flynn did nothing. Perhaps they were too shocked by what had happened. Perhaps he was simply no longer of use to them.

"*Turn around.*" The voice was only a whisper, but Bart turned – and found a small skiff had drawn up behind him.

A pair of gloved hands reached out to him. Without a moment's hesitation, Bart lifted Connor forward, drawing on the last of his strength. The hands helped pull Connor out of the water and into the small boat. Bart made the mistake of looking down, and saw a spiral of blood rising up through the water. He felt a fin brush past his feet . . . But then the hands reached out once more and, at last, he too was safely inside the boat.

Bart looked up, gratefully, towards his saviour – but the face was entirely hidden by a dark mask.

"*You are tired, friend,*" came the whisper again. "*You fought so well but now you must rest.*"

"Who are you?" Bart asked. He did feel immensely tired and his eyelids were already half closed.

His rescuer did not reply; simply turned and took up the oars. As he did so, Bart spotted another passenger by his feet.

"Jez!" he exclaimed.

"*He is sleeping now,*" said the mysterious ferryman. "*So is Connor. And now, so too must you. We'll meet again in time, Bart. I owe you a debt of thanks.*"

How does he know our names? thought Bart, searching the mask for clues. But there was nothing. No longer able to stave off the deep tiredness, he slumped back against the side of the boat and closed his eyes. He fell instantly asleep.

"*Safe now,*" said the masked boatman, as he steered the skiff swiftly away from Hell Bay.

CHAPTER TWELVE

Surfacing

Connor opened his eyes and found himself staring up into the blinding lights of *Calle del Marinero*.

He was lying on the deck of the small light-boat. His head felt foggy and, as he twisted to his side and found Bart and Jez lying beside him, a sharp pain seared through his skull. His groans woke the others.

"Where are we?" asked Bart, completely disorientated.

"*Calle del Marinero*," said Connor.

"What day is it?" asked Jez.

"Never mind that," said Bart. "Why are we only wearing underwear? Where have all our clothes gone?"

It was a good question but, as hard as he tried to think back, Connor couldn't remember.

Bart's face suddenly turned a livid shade of green. "I think I'm going to throw up now," he said quite calmly, leaning over the side of the boat.

Connor grinned and shook his head. "Ouch!" He must remember not to do that again in a hurry.

"That's better!" said Bart, wiping his mouth clean.

"Charming," said Jez.

65

Connor managed to heave himself up into a sitting position. As he did so, he saw that, in the distance, a familiar ship was approaching the floating city. "It's *The Diablo*," Connor said. "They've come to pick us up!"

"Already?" said Bart.

"Must be Sunday night, then," said Jez.

"I suppose so," said Connor. "Do either of you remember exactly how we spent our shore leave?"

Jez shook his head. Bart looked equally dumbstruck. Then he broke into a smile. "That must have been some shore leave, eh? For us to be half-naked and not remember a thing!"

"I guess," Connor said. Suddenly, he noticed something. "Look," he said, with a smile. "I got a tattoo." He held out the inside of his forearm. There was a picture of three cutlasses, their hilts intertwined. Beneath the artwork, his skin was red and tender but, that aside, it looked good!

Bart and Jez extended their own arms.

"Hey," said Bart. "Look, we all got one!"

"They're exactly the same!" said Jez, examining his forearm.

"Well *almost* exactly," Connor said. "Look, Bart's got an extra bit on his. Just below the swords."

The others looked more closely.

"He's right," said Bart. "What is that?"

"It's a letter," Jez said. "The letter K."

Bart looked at it, puzzled. "Why K?"

Jez shook his head. "Search me!"

"I don't know either," Connor said. It was a mystery. "It's a cool tattoo though, isn't it?"

Jez grinned. "It's a souvenir of The Three Buccaneers' first shore leave together!"

"Let's hope we remember more of the next one, eh?" said Bart. "By the way, does anyone else's head feel like it's being split open like a clam?"

"Yes!" cried Jez and Connor simultaneously.

"One for all . . ." said Bart softly.

"And all for one!" answered the others in little more than a whisper.

The Diablo had come into its mooring just a little further out in the bay. It would be easier to steer the light-boat towards it than for the larger ship to come closer into the harbour.

Bart unfastened the ropes tying the small boat to its mooring, and cast them off. Connor took up the tiller once more. As he turned to take a last look at *Calle del Marinero*, the pain in his head suddenly intensified. He shut his eyes, just for a second. In that moment, a strange jumble of images raced through his mind. *A dingy bar. Two hands locked together. Wheels. A beautiful ship. Playing cards. Grace's face. Danger. Underwater. The face of a girl. The flap of a tail. Magic. Underwater. A stingray. A shoal of yellow fish. And then . . . darkness.*

He opened his eyes again, trying to keep hold of the images but unable to. They were replaced by Bart's grin.

"Here's a little tip for you, buddy. You might find it easier to steer a straight course with your eyes open." Bart shrugged. "Just a thought."

Connor took hold of the tiller and set his course towards *The Diablo*. His first, mysterious, shore leave was officially over.

*

67

Out in the ocean, a sleek windjammer drifts in the darkness.

Sidorio surveys the deck of *The Lorelei*. The surviving fishtails sit slumped in their chairs. They look weak and wretched. Blood drips from more than one of their oilskins.

"Now," Sidorio says. "I heard word you needed a new captain and, lucky you, I'm available to take up the post right away."

He is unfazed by the looks of contempt emanating from Kally, Teahan, Lika and the other survivors. Contempt is just one step away from respect in Sidorio's book. He smiles.

"I was impressed with you lot today," he says. "I can see you could be quite a tricky bunch if you raise your game just a notch. You have a few nifty moves. Nice appetite for violence, too. We can work on that, crank it up to the next level."

He turns, seeing Flynn hobble along the deck towards him – a broken man. Sidorio shakes his head. "I don't think we'll have much need of you, though, Grandpa. Not in the new scheme of things." He chuckles. "You make yourself comfortable and we'll work out what we do with you later."

Sidorio looks at the rest of them. He can sense he has their full and undivided attention now. They are petrified of him. Just the way he likes it.

This is the beginning of a new journey. It is an invigorating thought. After all these years at sea – these endless years – Sidorio's true voyage is at last ready to begin. It's as if he has woken from the deepest of sleeps. As if he has swum up from the darkest of depths. And before he rests again, everyone who navigates the oceans will know his name. Know it, respect it, *fear* it.

There is much work to be done.

The Vampirates will return in . . . *Blood Captain*.

☠ WIN ☠

Your portrait in the style of a Vampirate by illustrator Bob Lea

One lucky winner will win a fantastic and unique MONEY CAN'T BUY
prize – a portrait of you as a flamboyant Vampirate character
by Vampirates illustrator Bob Lea!

To enter, log on to www.vampirates.co.uk, tear out or photocopy
this page, filling in your answers on the reverse, and send it to:

**World Book Day Vampirates Competition
Marketing Department
Simon and Schuster Children's Books
Africa House, 64-78 Kingsway, London WC2B 6AH**

Simply answer the questions below and tell us what name
you'd give yourself as a character in the Vampirates crew:

1. Who are the Three Buccaneers?
2. What is Kally's full name?
3. Who is the author of the Vampirates books?

My Vampirate name would be: _____

My (real) name: _____

My age: _____

My parent/guardian's signature: _____
(you must get your parent/guardian's signature if you are under 12 years old)

My telephone no: _____

My address: _____

Postcode: _____